Prince

Cinderella

STARRING

Fairy God-
mother

Stepmother

Anastasia

Drizella

This edition published by Parragon Books Ltd in 2014

Parragon Books Ltd
Chartist House
15–17 Trim Street
Bath BA1 1HA, UK
www.parragon.com

ISBN 978-1-4723-2389-7
Printed in China

Cinderella

Bath · New York · Cologne · Melbourne · Delhi
Hong Kong · Shenzhen · Singapore · Amsterdam

Once upon a time, in a faraway land, there lived a rich, widowed gentleman and his beautiful daughter, Cinderella.

Cinderella's father was kind and loving. He married for a second time so that his daughter had a mother to care for her.

Cinderella's stepmother had two mean and ugly daughters called Anastasia and Drizella.

When Cinderella's father died, her
stepmother stopped pretending to like her.
She was jealous of Cinderella's charm and
beauty so she forced the young girl to
become a servant in her own home.

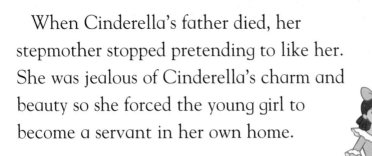

Cinderella was given a tiny bedroom in the attic. Her
only friends were the birds and mice. They listened as she
sang about her dreams of a life filled with happiness.

One morning, Cinderella found a tubby little mouse caught in a trap. "We'll call you Gus," she said. Then she gently set him free and put him with the other mice for safety. "Don't forget to warn him about Lucifer!" Cinderella reminded them. And off she went to begin the day's chores.

Lucifer was her stepmother's cat. He was sly and lazy, and all the animals hated him, especially Bruno the dog.

After Cinderella had given Lucifer his milk, she walked out into the yard. "Breakfast time!" she called, scattering corn for the chickens.

The mice came running for some breakfast too. But Lucifer was blocking the way to the corn. One of the mice, Jaq, crept bravely up to Lucifer and kicked him. There was a loud –
SPLASH! The cat had fallen into his milk bowl.

This made Lucifer very angry. When he saw Gus busily gathering up some of the corn, he pounced on him…

Luckily, Gus managed to escape to the kitchen. He scampered up onto a table top where he rested against a teacup. Suddenly, the cup flipped over, trapping Gus underneath.

Just then, a voice shrieked from upstairs. "Cinderella!"

"I'm coming," Cinderella sighed. She picked up the breakfast trays and made her way upstairs. Under the teacup, Gus was safe at last.

Not far away, in the royal palace, the King and Grand Duke were talking about the Prince.

"It's time he married," grumbled the King. Suddenly, he had an idea. "We'll have a ball – tonight!" he cried. "And invite every young maiden in the kingdom. The Prince will surely fall in love with one of them!"

So, invitations were sent out that very day.

When the royal messenger delivered the invitation to Cinderella's house, Cinderella went to find her stepmother. She was upstairs in the music room listening to Anastasia and Drizella singing.

"There's going to be a ball at the palace!" exclaimed the stepmother as she read the invitation. "Every young maiden is to attend!"

"Why, that means I can go too!" said Cinderella, hopefully.

Anastasia and Drizella shrieked with laughter at the idea, but Cinderella was determined. "Well, why not?" she asked.

Her stepmother thought for a moment, then a sly look crossed her face.

"I see no reason why you can't go, if you get all your work done."

"I'm sure I can!" cried Cinderella, rushing upstairs to find something to wear.

She opened her wardrobe and took out one of her mother's old gowns. "It's a little old-fashioned, but I'll fix that," she said.

"Cinderella!" shrieked her stepmother.

"I'm coming," Cinderella sighed.

The mice knew that poor Cinderella would never have time to finish the dress. So they decided to work on it themselves.

They sang merrily as they cut and sewed the material. At last, the pretty dress was finished. It was trimmed with an old sash and beads which Anastasia and Drizella had thrown away.

Later that evening, Cinderella sadly returned to her attic room. She had been so busy that she hadn't had time to get ready. Out of the window, she watched a carriage arrive to take her stepmother and stepsisters to the ball.

As Cinderella turned away she suddenly saw the dress. "Surprise!" her friends cried.

"Oh, it's wonderful!" Cinderella exclaimed, hardly able to believe her eyes. In no time at all, she had slipped the dress on and was rushing downstairs to the carriage.

But when Anastasia and Drizella saw their stepsister looking so beautiful, they were filled with jealousy.

"Why, you little thief!" Drizella screamed, spotting her old beads around Cinderella's neck. Then, Anastasia looked at the sash. "That's mine!" she cried, grabbing the sash and ripping Cinderella's dress.

"Please, stop!" cried Cinderella. But it was too late, her dress was ruined. She ran into the garden and flung herself down by a bench. She sobbed as if her heart would break.

Cinderella was so upset that at first she didn't see a magical swirl of light gather around her. When she looked up, an old lady was sitting on the bench.

"I'm your fairy godmother," the lady said, kindly. "Dry your tears. You can't go to the ball looking like that! Now, fetch me a pumpkin, and hurry, even miracles take time!"

Minutes later, the fairy godmother waved her magic wand over the pumpkin. "*Bibbidi-bobbidi-booo*!" she sang. The pumpkin changed into a sparkling carriage!

"Now," said the fairy godmother, "with an elegant carriage like that, you simply have to have – mice!"

With that, she waved her wand over Gus, Jaq and their friends and changed them into proud, white horses. Another wave of the wand and Cinderella's horse was changed into a coachman and Bruno the dog was changed into a footman.

Then, with a final wave of the wand, Cinderella was dressed
in a magnificent ball gown and delicate glass slippers.

"Oh, thank you!" cried Cinderella, stepping into the
carriage. "It's like a dream coming true!"

"I know, dear, but remember you only have until midnight,"
the fairy godmother warned. "On the last stroke of twelve the
spell will be broken."

At the palace, Cinderella entered the glittering ballroom excitedly.

Glancing up, the Prince saw her and thought she was the most beautiful girl he had ever seen. He took Cinderella's hand and led her to the dance floor. The Prince knew that he had finally fallen in love.

Dancing in the Prince's arms, Cinderella felt as though she were floating on air.

Suddenly, she heard a
clock chime. It was the first
stroke of midnight…

"I must go!" Cinderella gasped as she fled through the
ballroom and down the palace steps.

"Wait! You can't go now!" cried the Prince. But Cinderella
didn't stop – even when she lost one of her glass slippers on
the steps. She leapt into the carriage, which raced away.

As the last stroke of midnight was heard, the carriage turned back into a pumpkin and Cinderella found herself dressed in rags once more. But she was still wearing a single, glass slipper.

Back at the palace, the Prince was heartbroken. He declared he would marry only the girl whose foot fitted the glass slipper he had found.

The next day, the Grand Duke began his search. Every maiden in the land would have to try on the glass slipper until he found the Prince's true love.

Meanwhile, Cinderella's stepmother had become suspicious
when she heard her stepdaughter humming the music from the
ball. She was determined that Cinderella would not try on the
slipper. When Cinderella went up to her room, she followed
her and locked the door!

At last, the Grand Duke arrived. Anastasia and Drizella were very excited. Taking their turn, they tried to *s-q-u-e-e-z-e* their feet into the tiny, glass slipper. But their feet were much too big.

Jaq and Gus were desperate to help Cinderella. They took the attic key from the stepmother's pocket and slowly pushed it up the stairs to Cinderella's room.

Hot and tired, they finally managed to open the door and free their friend.

Just as the Grand Duke was about to leave, Cinderella appeared. "Please, wait!" she called. "May I try on the slipper?"

The Grand Duke led Cinderella to a chair and called for the footman. As the footman stepped forward, the wicked stepmother tripped him up. The slipper flew through the air. There was a loud crash as it hit the floor and shattered into a thousand tiny pieces.

"Oh, no!" gasped the Duke.

"Perhaps this would help…" said Cinderella, reaching into her pocket and bringing out the other glass slipper. Her stepsisters shrieked as the delighted Duke fitted the slipper onto Cinderella's foot.

Soon afterwards, Cinderella and the Prince were married.
Her friends, the mice, looked on and smiled. They knew
Cinderella's dreams had finally come true!